GUM GIRL

★ ★ IN ★ ★

MUSIC, MISCHIEF AND MAYHEM!

ANDI WATSON

WALKER

To Carlotta

First published 2013 by Walker Books Ltd

87 Vauxhall Walk, London SE11 5HJ

2 4 6 8 10 9 7 5 3 1

Text & Illustrations © 2013 Andi Watson

The right of Andi Watson to be identified as author of this work has been asserted by him
in accordance with the Copyright, Designs and Patents Act 1988

This book has been typeset in Block T

Printed and bound in Malaysia

British Library Cataloguing in Publication Data: a catalogue record for this
book is available from the British Library

ISBN 978-1-4063-2942-1

www.walker.co.uk   www.gumgirl.co.uk

7

8

10

13

14

16

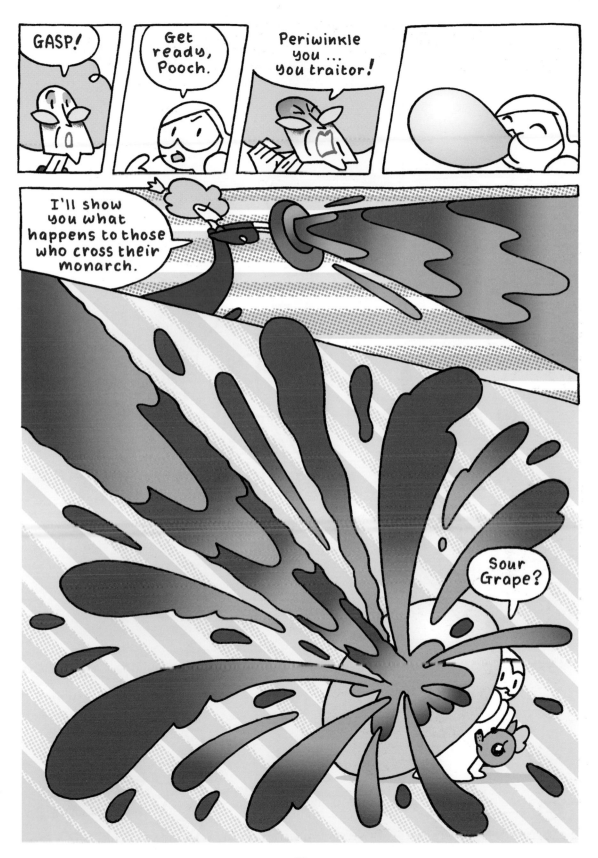

26

27

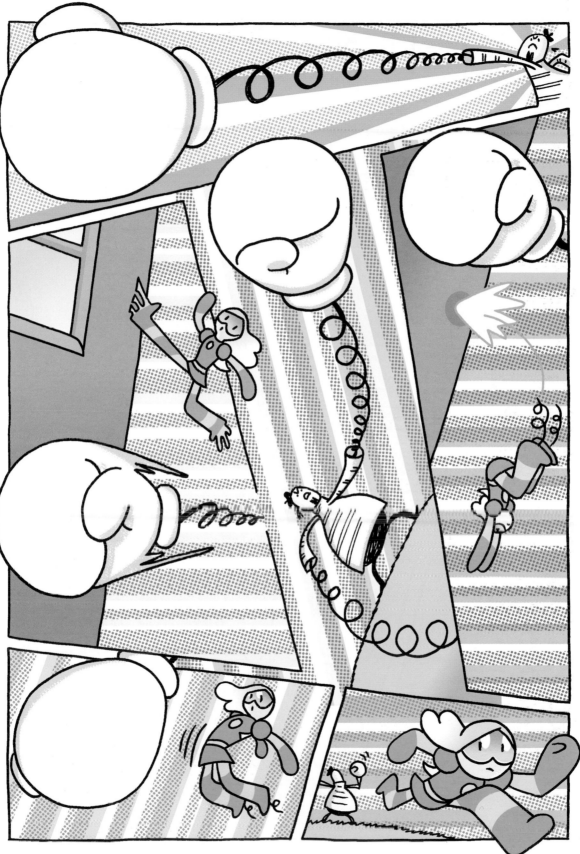

36

40

41

46

47

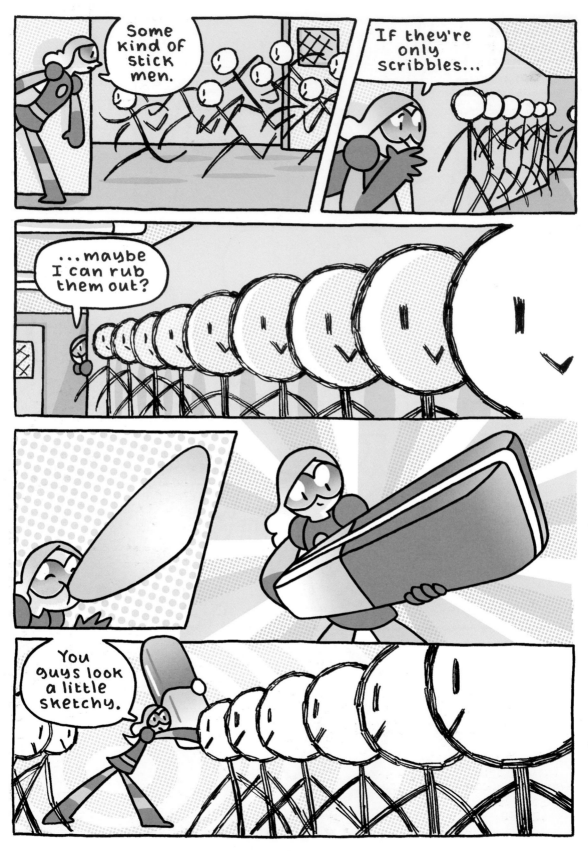

54

59

60